Omar's Halloween

Maryann Kovalski

Fitzhenry & Whiteside

Published in Canada by Fitzhenry & Whiteside,
195 Allstate Parkway, Markham, Ontario L3R 4T8

Published in the United States by Fitzhenry & Whiteside,
311 Washington Street, Brighton, Massachusetts 02135

www.fitzhenry.ca godwit@fitzhenry.ca

10 9 8 7 6 5 4 3 2 1

Library and Archives Canada Cataloguing in Publication

Kovalski, Maryann
Omar's Halloween / Maryann Kovalski.

ISBN 1-55041-559-X

I. Title.

PS8571.O96O53 2006 jC813'.54 C2006-900079-4

U.S. Publisher Cataloging-in-Publication Data
(Library of Congress Standards)

Kovalski, Maryann.
Omar's Halloween / Maryann Kovalski.
[32] p. : col. ill. ; cm.
Summary: As Halloween arrives, and Omar still hasn't found a costume scary enough, he is forced to put a sheet over his head and trick-or-treat as a boring old ghost. Omar's Halloween is ruined _ until the weather comes to his aid.
ISBN 1-55041-559-X
1. Halloween _ Fiction. I. Title.
[E] 22 PZ7.K85655Om 2006

Fitzhenry & Whiteside acknowledges with thanks the Canada Council for the Arts, and the Ontario Arts Council for their support of our publishing program. We acknowledge the financial support of the Government of Canada through the Book Publishing Industry Development Program (BPIDP) for our publishing activities.

Canada Council for the Arts Conseil des Arts du Canada

Cover and Book Design by Wycliffe Smith Design
Printed in Hong Kong.

Omar's Halloween

For Greg,
Genny and
Joanna

Black cats howled. Wind moaned. Halloween was coming.

Happy
Halloween
Please come
Please come to my
Thomas
Please
Please come to my party
Elsie
Please
Come to
my party
Bart
Please come
Joel
Please
come
Please
come

Omar couldn't wait. After trick-or-treating, the party would be at his house. He and his friends would bob for apples and tell ghost stories. And he would wear the scariest costume.

Omar's mother was going to make him a spider costume. The thought of all those hairy legs made Omar shiver. He liked that.

Maybe somebody would faint.

There would never be another Halloween like this one.

"I am going to be a spider," said Omar to Elsie at the pumpkin patch.

"That will be fun," she said.

"And scary," said Omar.

"Not a bit," she said. "Spiders are helpful. They eat mosquitoes and the bugs that hurt the farmers' crops."

"Oh," said Omar. "I didn't know that."

"Why don't you be a ghost?" said Elsie. "They're scary."

Omar didn't want to be a ghost. Ghosts weren't the worst kind of scary.

When Omar shopped for the party, he spotted the perfect costume—a bat! Sometimes at night, he saw them swooping. Bats made him shiver.

Thomas was shopping for a costume, too.

"I'm going to be a bat!" said Omar.

"Bats are amazing," said Thomas.

"So scary!" said Omar.

"Not at all," said Thomas. "They're great flyers, and they catch nasty bugs."

"Oh," said Omar. "I didn't know that." He put the bat costume back on the shelf.

At the end of the day, Omar had everything he needed for the party—except a costume.

On the afternoon of Halloween, the street was quiet. Everyone was inside getting dressed up. Some jack-o'-lanterns

were already lit. Behind every door, treats were piled high. Everyone was ready for the big night…

...except Omar.

He tried on his dad's hat and coat, which made him look like Omar in his dad's hat and coat.

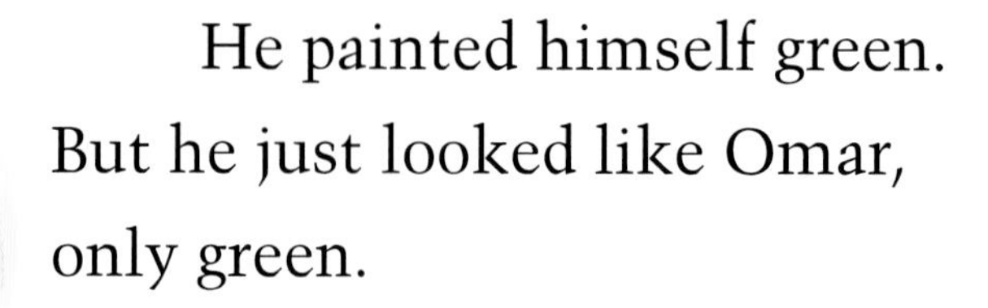

He painted himself green. But he just looked like Omar, only green.

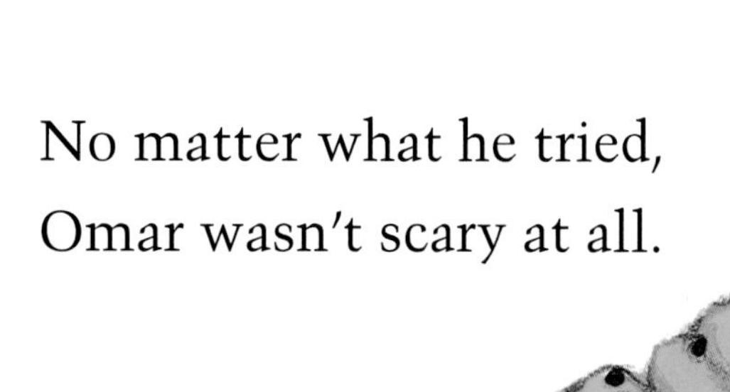

No matter what he tried, Omar wasn't scary at all.

He wasn't anything at all.

He watched the first trick-or-treaters from his window.

"It's Halloween, and I have no costume," said Omar sadly.

"Yes, you do!" cried his mother, who sailed down the stairs with a billowy sheet. "You will scare everyone tonight," she said. And she slipped the ghost costume over his head.

The doorbell rang. Thomas, his dad, and Elsie arrived to take Omar trick-or-treating. Everyone agreed that a ghost costume was perfectly scary for Halloween.

But Omar didn't agree.

TRICK
OR
TREAT

Outside, the street was full of ghosts. At every house, Omar heard the same thing.

"Oh, look! Another cute ghost!"

No one was even a little frightened of Omar.

"This Halloween can't get worse," said Omar.

He was wrong.

The first rain plops sent everyone scattering. Their bags were full, and they were ready for the party. They giggled and shrieked as they ran for Omar's house.

Omar tried to run, too. But his legs got all tangled in the sheet.

The others ran ahead. The rain came down harder. Omar tripped and fell into a thorny bush. He called his friends to stop. But they were far ahead, and the wind gobbled up his words.

Omar dragged himself out of the bush.

Omar ran as fast as he could on the muddy ground. He didn't see the pumpkins that sent him sliding down a gully, into a cold puddle.

With all his might, Omar hauled himself up and trudged toward the glowing lights of home.

Omar stood outside his window and watched his party. Elsie got an apple and everyone cheered. It was nice to see his friends have fun in his house.

Who cares if I don't have the scariest costume? thought Omar. *I can still have a good time at my party.*

He knocked on the door, but nobody heard him. He knocked again, harder. He knocked until his mother finally opened the door.

HA
HALL

BOO!

Omar's mother gasped. "Who—
or what...is it?"

Omar oozed through the door and watched it happen.

Elsie shrieked first. Thomas hid under the sofa. Bart quivered behind the curtains. Omar's parents held each other tight to keep themselves from fainting.

It was Omar's happiest Halloween.

Later that night, Omar said to his mother, "There will never be another Halloween like that one."

"Oh, good," she answered.

HAPPY HALLOWEEN